Time to Go, Hippo!

To Joshua B.H.
To John and Pamela, with love K.S.

Text copyright © 1999 Bob Hartman
Illustrations copyright © 1999 Kate Simpson
This edition copyright © 1999 Lion Publishing

The moral rights of the author and illustrator
have been asserted

Published by
Lion Publishing plc
Sandy Lane West, Oxford, England
www.lion-publishing.co.uk
ISBN 0 7459 4162 1
Lion Publishing
4050 Lee Vance View, Colorado Springs,
CO 80918, USA
ISBN 0 7459 4162 1

First edition 1999
10 9 8 7 6 5 4 3 2 1 0

A catalogue record for this book is available
from the British Library

Library of Congress CIP data applied for

Typeset in 16/24 Baskerville MT Schoolbook
Printed and bound in Malaysia

Time to Go, Hippo!

Bob Hartman

Illustrations by
Kate Simpson

LION
Children's Books

'There's a monster in the rice field!' the farmers shouted, as they ran back, terrified, into town. 'It's trampling our crops!'

'A monster?' asked the mayor. 'What does it look like?'

And all the farmers talked at once:

'It has stomping feet!'

'And chomping teeth!'

'And it's big and bumpy and grey!'

'It sounds like a hippopotamus,' came a voice from the crowd. It was Barnabas, the old monk who lived out in the desert.

'Not a monster — a hippo!' the old man repeated.

'But it has stomping feet!'

'And chomping teeth!'

'And it's big and bumpy and grey!'

'Then we must drive it away!' announced the mayor. 'Grab your weapons, everyone!'

But old Barnabas just shook his head. 'It's only a hippo,' he sighed. 'I hope they don't hurt it.'

The farmers held their weapons high:
wheat-thrashers and rat-smashers, hay-slashers
and potato-mashers, broomsticks and rakes and
clubs.

'Time to go, hippo!' the mayor shouted.

But the beast just stood there and blinked.

And so the farmers charged, waving their
wheat-thrashers and shaking their hay-slashers
and swinging their broomsticks and clubs.

Patiently, the hippo watched the farmers.
Calmly, he stopped his chewing.

Then, suddenly, he opened wide his mouth
and he ROARED! And the sound of that roar
was so terrible that it filled the heart of every
farmer with fear!

They dropped their rat-smashers, they flung
away their potato-mashers, and they ran back,
terrified, into town.

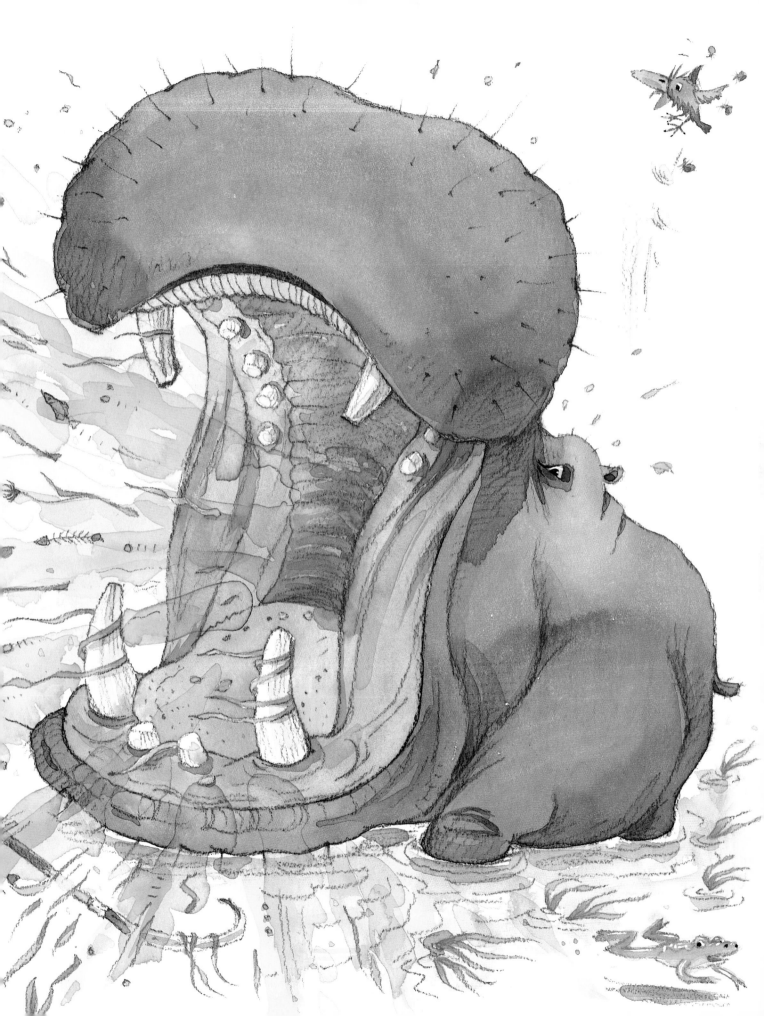

'Stomping feet!' they panted.

'Chomping teeth!' they puffed.

'Big and bumpy and NOISY and grey!'

'But it's just a hippo,' old Barnabas said. 'Perhaps I can help.'

'Nonsense!' shouted the mayor. 'You're no match for that monster. What we need are… the HOUNDS!'

And so the townspeople brought out their beasts: beagles and bassets, boxers and bloodhounds, and one big bad bulldog!

'This is not right!' old Barnabas protested. 'These are all God's creatures. And some of them… some of them are going to get hurt!'

But the mayor ignored him.

'Off to the hunt!' he shouted.

When the animals had reached the field,
the mayor shouted again, 'Time to go, hippo!'
But still the hippo would not budge.

And so, barking and baying, yipping and
yapping, and baring their sharp white teeth,
the hounds raced towards the hippo.

Patiently, the hippo watched them.

Calmly, he stopped his chewing.

Then, once again, he opened wide his mouth and he ROARED. And the force of that roar was so powerful that it sent the beasts flying!

Beagles and bassets, bloodhounds and boxers, and one big bad bulldog went sailing back across the field, over the crowd and into the middle of town.

'Stomping feet!' cried the townspeople.

'Chomping teeth!' they gasped.

'Big and bumpy and POWERFUL and grey!' But old Barnabas just sighed, as a basset went bouncing by.

'The army!' cried the mayor. 'We must call out the army!'

So messengers were sent and, in no time, the army arrived: generals and majors, corporals and captains, with catapults and chariots and battering-rams!

Barnabas shook his old head. 'Please,' he begged, 'let me try to get rid of the hippo — before somebody else gets hurt.'

'I shouldn't worry about that,' the mayor grinned. 'That hippo has met his match.'

And he marched off with the army to the rice field.

'Time to go, hippo!' the mayor called to the beast. But again the hippo kept on chewing, as if nothing at all had happened.

And so the soldiers charged across the field: aiming their catapults, and racing their chariots, and heaving high their battering-rams.

Patiently, the hippo watched them.

Calmly, he stopped his chewing.

And then, once more, he opened wide his mouth and ROARED. And the smell of that roar was so foul that it turned the bravest soldier green!

Back raced the generals and the majors, back raced the corporals and captains — back into town, far from that awful smell!

'I've had enough of this,' Barnabas sighed. And he hurried to the market-place where he begged two tiny potatoes, a couple of plump parsnips and some large yellow onions. Then he picked up his sturdy wooden staff and set off to the rice field.

On the way, he passed the mayor.

'Stomping feet!' he moaned.

'Chomping teeth!' he wept.

'Big and bumpy and SMELLY and grey.'

'I know,' Barnabas nodded. 'But I think I can make him go away.'

Barnabas prayed a little prayer and walked
slowly across the field. As he walked, he stuck
the potatoes in his ears and pushed the parsnips
up his nose.

Then he planted the staff as firmly as
he could into the soft ground and held
on for dear life.

Patiently, the hippo watched him.

Calmly, he stopped his chewing.

And then, not once, not twice, but three times, he ROARED.

But because Barnabas had squeezed the spuds into his ears, the noisy roar did not scare him. And because he had poked the parsnips up his nose, the smelly roar did not offend him. And because he had stuck his stick into the ground, the powerful roar did not blow him away.

'Now then,' he said to the hippo, when the
roaring had stopped, 'it's time for us to talk.'

A few minutes later, the old man and the hippo walked back from the field together, until they reached the trembling mayor.

'How did you do it?' asked the mayor. 'How did you make the hippo move?'

'It was simple,' the old monk said. 'I told him we were sorry for the way we had treated him. I explained that we were all God's creatures and that it's important for us to get along — so he needed to leave your rice alone and go back to where he belonged.'

'Finally,' and here the old man grinned and reached into his pouch, 'I offered him one of these.'

'An onion?' said the mayor.

'Hippos love them!' Barnabas beamed. 'It's something I discovered by watching them. Something I never would have learned by chasing them away.'

And with that, he popped another onion into his new friend's mouth.

'Time to go, hippo,' said Barnabas gently.
And the old monk and the 'monster' walked off
into the desert.